THE ADVENTURES OF OFFICER BYRD™
GET HELP!

Inspired from a True Story!

Created & Written by Michael Simonsen
Story by Michael Simonsen & Stephanus Dharma
Illustrated by Stephanus Dharma
Edited by Bill Couch

**OFFICER BYRD
PUBLISHING CO.**
WWW.OFFICERBYRD.ORG

Officer Byrd Publishing Company,
15730 Williams Circle, Lake Mathews CA 92570.
Library Of Congress Control Number 2006935597
ISBN 0-978-7322-00
THE ADVENTURES OF OFFICER BYRD
Written and Created by Michael Simonsen
Illustrated by Stephanus Dharma
First printed in 2007

Printed in China

INTRODUCTION

This book is dedicated to all the children that have been abused. If you are seeking help, please get help and remember none of this is your fault. To the adults that have been abused and have not talked about it, now it's your time to get help and know that it was never your fault.

This book is dedicated to all the real heroes, police officers, paramedics, social workers, and people who help those children and adults to get help and make them feel safer. I dedicate this book to Officer Byrd who has taught many children to be safe and happy. Also to my family, my wife and children who have been patient while I wrote this book.

To my illustrator, Stephanus, who has brought life through his imagination and illustrations to "The Adventures of Officer Byrd." To the Los Angeles Police Department where I was proud to protect and serve as a Police Officer and to the other police officers who help children and adults every day.

To Jim Kling who gave me Officer Byrd and helped me train him. To Terrie Jones who helped proof read the book and Bill Couch who edited the book.

Thank you Taylor for using your likeness in this book.

To Greg Healey and Tim Grass of www.TwoWebGuys.com for creating www.OfficerByrd.org website.

To you for buying this book, because your donation is going to help The Officer Byrd Non Profit Org., to open Officer Byrd Safe Houses for abused children.

OFFICER MIKE   OFFICER BYRD

This story starts in
the jungles of South America.
In a tree are three
blue and gold macaws (parrots).
Dad, Mom and their son named Byrd.

Dad and Mom are
teaching Byrd how to fly.
"Mom, Dad, I'm flying, Yeah!"
Mom and Dad are so proud of Byrd.

As Byrd is flying around the jungle, he sees two men approaching the tree where his Mom and Dad are. Mom and Dad don't see the men. The men reach up with two long nets and capture Mom and Dad.

Byrd is scared and swoops down
to help his Mom and Dad.
Byrd accidentally hits a branch and falls
to the ground not too far from the men and
his parents. Byrd is dizzy and can't
move his body for a while.

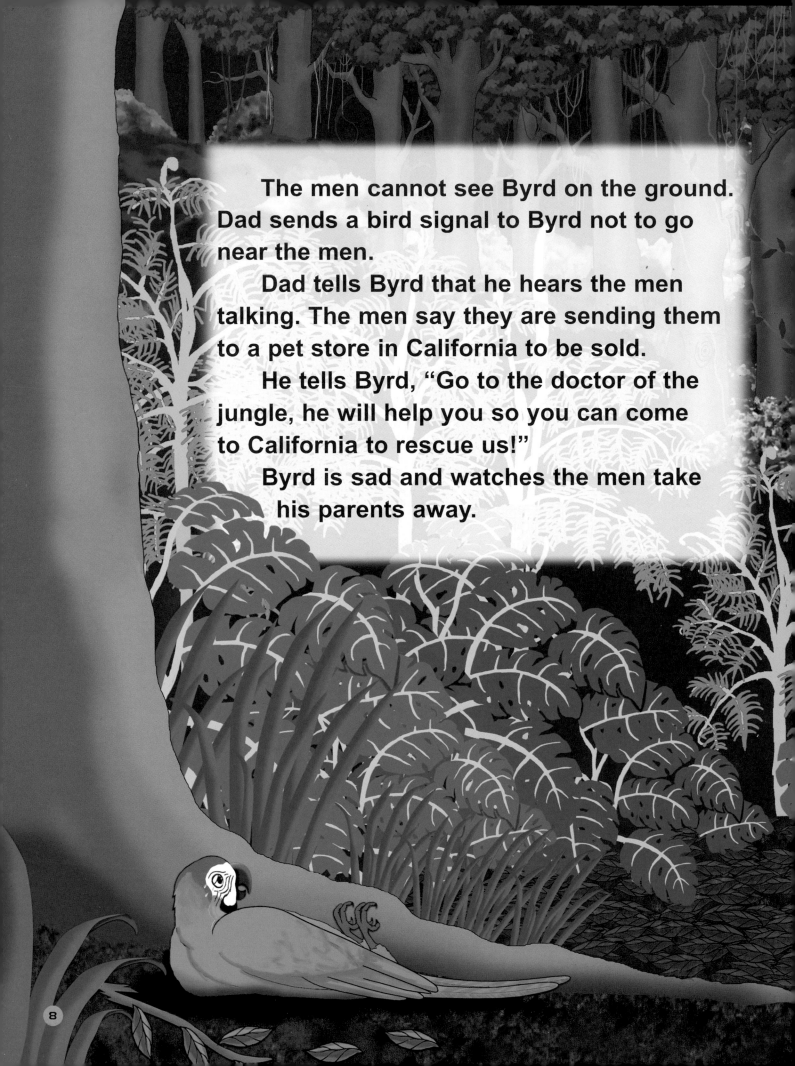

The men cannot see Byrd on the ground. Dad sends a bird signal to Byrd not to go near the men.

Dad tells Byrd that he hears the men talking. The men say they are sending them to a pet store in California to be sold.

He tells Byrd, "Go to the doctor of the jungle, he will help you so you can come to California to rescue us!"

Byrd is sad and watches the men take his parents away.

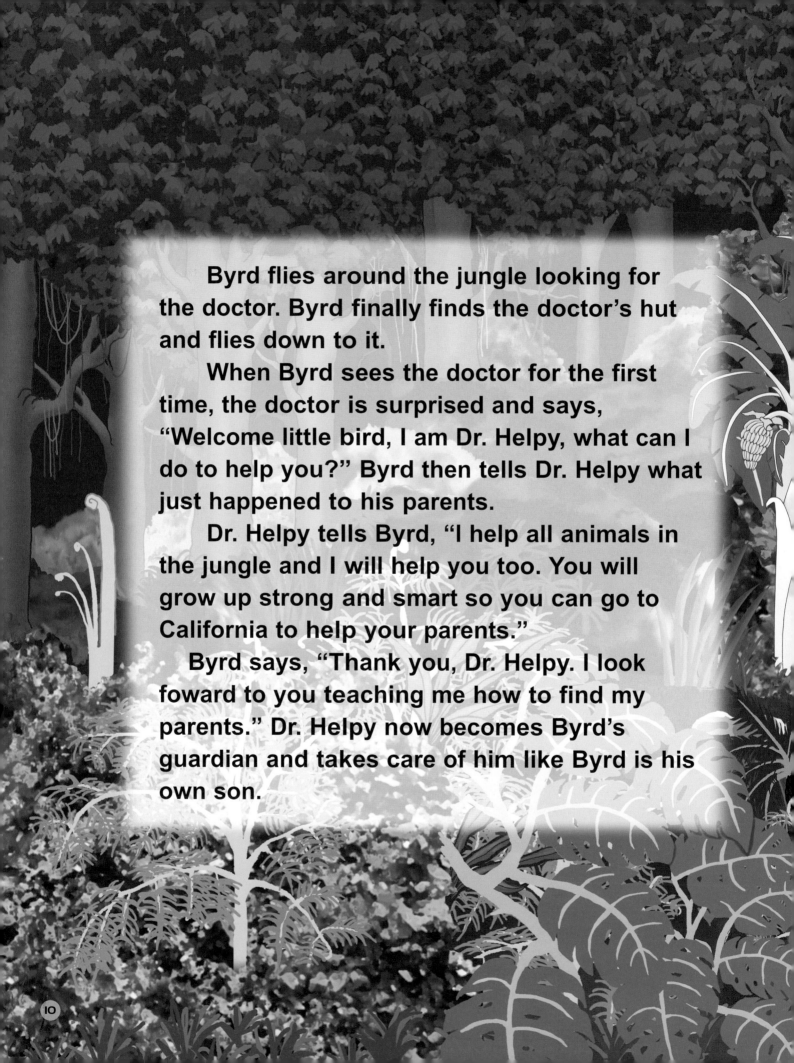

Byrd flies around the jungle looking for the doctor. Byrd finally finds the doctor's hut and flies down to it.

When Byrd sees the doctor for the first time, the doctor is surprised and says, "Welcome little bird, I am Dr. Helpy, what can I do to help you?" Byrd then tells Dr. Helpy what just happened to his parents.

Dr. Helpy tells Byrd, "I help all animals in the jungle and I will help you too. You will grow up strong and smart so you can go to California to help your parents."

Byrd says, "Thank you, Dr. Helpy. I look foward to you teaching me how to find my parents." Dr. Helpy now becomes Byrd's guardian and takes care of him like Byrd is his own son.

Dr. Helpy teaches Byrd how to be strong and how to defend himself.

Dr. Helpy says. "You will help animals, good people and kids too." Dr. Helpy also gives Byrd magic powers to help Byrd become super strong and be able to talk to humans.

Dr. Helpy tells Byrd, "Only use these powers when you need to fight bad guys and bad animals or to help others who need your help. Find a good human to work with you. Tell him the story about your parents and about your powers."

Dr. Helpy tells Byrd, "Go back to your home because those men who kidnapped your parents will be coming back. They want more parrots to take to California. Be safe and happy."

Byrd says goodbye to Dr. Helpy and thanks him for all the care and knowledge he gave him.

After waiting for several days, Byrd sees the same men coming and lets himself be captured.

Byrd is kept in a box and taken away on a boat to be shipped to California. Byrd is happy and anxious that he's going to help his parents. After several days, Byrd arrives in California and he is taken to a pet store, but his parents are not there.

Officer Mike, a Police Officer for the Los Angeles Police Department, is assigned to patrol the streets of Los Angeles. He also talks to elementary schools kids about safety. Officer Mike would talk about bicycling skateboarding, roller-skating, stranger danger and other safety subjects.

Sometimes Officer Mike has a rough time getting his message across to kids at the schools. Officer Mike wants the kids to listen better to him when he talks about the importance of safety.

Officer Mike thinks about how he can get the kids attention so they will listen and remember his safety talks.

Officer Mike decides to buy an animal to help him teach children to be safe. He goes to a local pet store and looks at all kinds of animals. Officer Mike looks at dogs, cats, snakes, spiders and even birds.

Byrd is sitting on top of a perch watching Officer Mike looking for a pet to buy. Byrd suddenly feels that this is the good human who can help find his parents.

**BUY 1 CAT
GET 1 DOG**

EARLY BIRD SPECIAL

Byrd flies to Officer Mike and starts to shake his head up and down. Officer Mike likes what Byrd was doing. Officer Mike tells the pet store owner that he wants Byrd to help him teach safety to children at the schools.

"Looks like the bird likes you Officer Mike," says Teresa, the owner of the store. She kindly gives Byrd to Officer Mike because she likes the idea that Byrd will be helping a police officer to teach kids about safety.

"Thank you so much Teresa, I will take good care of this bird and teach him to work with children," says Officer Mike.

Officer Mike is on patrol at the time he meets Byrd. Officer Mike takes Byrd to his patrol car and begins to patrol the streets until he can get Byrd home. Officer Mike suddenly receives a radio call of a bank robbery in progress on Main and Los Angeles Streets, which is located nearby. Officer Mike drives "Code Three", lights and sirens, to the bank.

When Officer Mike is about to jump out of the car to go to the bank, something remarkable happens. Byrd starts to talk! Byrd says, "Officer Mike, I can talk and understand humans and animals. I have special powers, so let me help you arrest the bad guys!"

He tells Officer Mike about Dr. Helpy who gave him magical powers. Byrd tells him about his mission to find his parents who were kidnapped.

Officer Mike is startled at first, then he tells Byrd, "Okay, I will help you find your parents and you can help me arrest the bad guys."

Officer Mike and Byrd go to the door of the bank and peek inside. Two men are pointing guns at people inside the bank. Officer Mike and Byrd hear one of the bank robbers shouting, "Give us the money or we will hurt all of you!" Officer Mike knows that he has to save the people in the bank immediately or they may get hurt.

Officer Mike tells Byrd, "Go through the airduct from the outside of the bank. When you get inside, distract the robbers and I will go through the front door and tell the robbers to drop their guns."

Officer Mike tells Byrd, "Be careful and safe, protect the people inside."

Byrd replies, "OK, let's get those bad guys." Byrd then flies to the roof and goes inside the airduct. He walks very quietly so the robbers won't hear his footsteps.

Officer Mike watches Byrd fly inside the bank and use his magical powers. Byrd suddenly becomes six feet tall and super strong.

Byrd flies in front of the robbers to protect the hostages. The robbers are stunned by Byrd and do not know what to do. The robbers then start to shoot at Byrd, but Byrd stops the bullets with his super strength.

One of the bank robbers tries to fight with Byrd, but Byrd jumps up and gives him a karate kick and knocks him down. Officer Mike tells the other robber, "DROP YOUR GUN!" Both robbers give up and are handcuffed by Officer Mike.

Officer Mike tells Byrd, "YOU ARE GREAT! I'm glad we're going to work together. Thank you for helping me! We're going to help a lot of people, especially kids."

Officer Mike puts the bank robbers in the police car. Byrd becomes small again and flies to Officer Mike's shoulder.

Everyone at the bank thanks Officer Mike and Byrd for saving their lives and gives them a big applause.

"You guys are heroes!" the people from the bank shout. Officer Mike says, "No we're not, we're just doing our job."

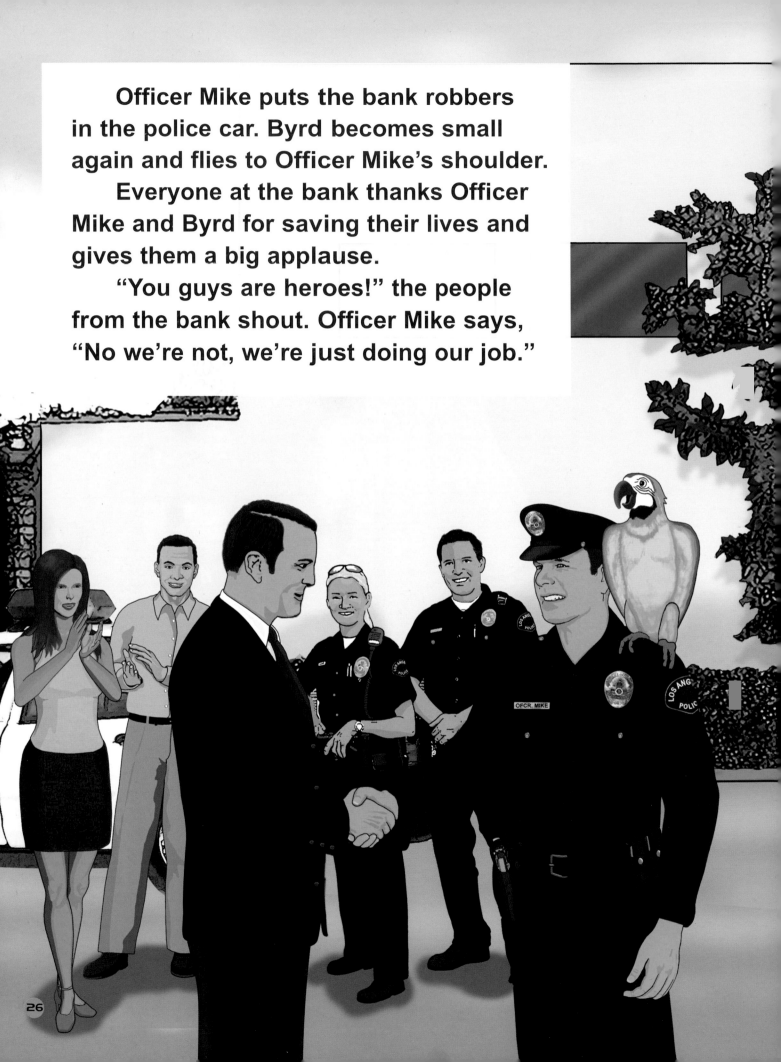

Officer Mike tells the Police Chief about how Byrd helped him capture the bank robbers. Officer Mike then tells the Chief that he wants to have Byrd as his partner to teach safety at schools.

The Police Chief honors Byrd by making Byrd a Police Officer with his very own badge. His badge number is 007. Officer Mike is very happy to have a new partner. From now on, Byrd is officially known as **OFFICER BYRD.**

Officer Byrd and Officer Mike have their first show at a school together in front of 500 elementary school kids. Officer Mike talks about the safety rules while Officer Byrd is riding his bike, skateboarding, and roller skating. The kids think that it's awesome to see that Officer Byrd can do the same things they do. All the kids think it's cool to see Officer Byrd playing basketball, throwing trash away, and driving a police car.

One of the things Officer Mike would teach the kids is, if anyone ever touched the private parts of their bodies, they should tell someone they trust. It doesn't matter if that person is a neighbor, friend, or family member, it is wrong to touch them on their privates. Officer Mike tells the kids if any body wanted to touch them in the wrong places, **SAY NO!** The person touching them in the wrong places is at fault. If that person threatened you not to say anything about what happened, you should tell someone you trust, like a friend, a teacher, a police officer, a firefighter or a family member. **GET HELP!** You will be safe when you **GET HELP!** This can happen to a boy or a girl. **GET HELP!**

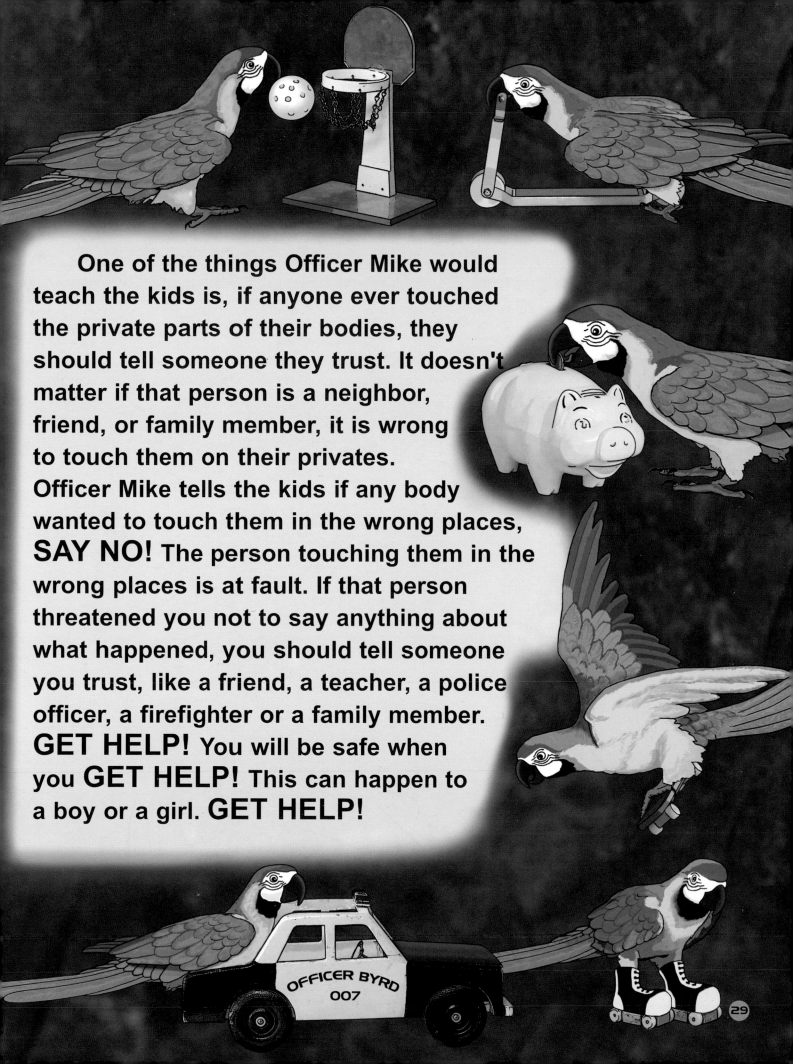

OFFICER BYRD
007

After the show, April tells her best friend Landon that her next door neighbor, Tom, baby sits her at his house. While her mom is at work, Tom, was touching her on her private parts. She is afraid to tell her mom or anyone else, because Tom told April he will hurt her and her mom if she tells anyone. April tells Landon she feels bad because of this. Landon says, "We should tell Officer Byrd so he could help you." April is so scared, and she tells Landon, "No!"

Landon knows that he has to help April and tells Officer Byrd who is still at the school.

Officer Byrd and Officer Mike meet with April's mom, Christine. Officer Mike tells Christine what Landon told them. Christine tells Officer Mike, "My neighbor Tom is helping me out and April's at Tom's house right now. I have to save my daughter!" Christine cries.

Officer Mike, Officer Byrd and Christine run to Tom's house. April and Tom are gone. They fear for April's life and think that Tom has kidnapped April.

Officer Byrd talks to the crows near Tom's house. The crows tell Officer Byrd that they saw Tom taking April in his car and driving to the freeway. Officer Byrd tells Officer Mike, who immediately calls for an "AMBER ALERT."

Officer Byrd and the crows fly in pursuit, to find and rescue April. Officer Byrd and the crows find Tom's car on the freeway. Officer Byrd then radios Officer Mike to follow them.

Officer Mike drives, "Code Three", lights and sirens, to where Tom and April are.

Officer Byrd uses his magical powers, becomes six feet tall and swoops down grabbing the top of the car, stopping it on the freeway. Officer Mike drives behind Tom's car.

Officer Byrd shouts, "Freeze, you're under arrest!"

Officer Byrd grabs Tom and takes him out of the car. Officer Byrd says, "You're under arrest and you will never hurt April again! You're a bad, bad, person!" Tom tries to get away, but Officer Byrd throws him to the ground. Officer Mike runs over to Tom and handcuffs him.

Officer Byrd returns to normal size and flies to Officer Mike's shoulder.

April is brought back to her mother. Officer Mike and Officer Byrd tell April, "You will be safe now, Tom will be going to jail. He will not hurt you or your mother ever again." Officer Mike says to April, "It is not your fault and you did nothing wrong."

"April, your mom will take you to a doctor to help you get through this terrible experience. You will be well and safe. You are a wonderful girl." Officer Byrd says.

Landon says, "YEAH, April is saved! Thank you Officer Byrd!"

The Beginning